Humming Hummingbird

Mary Elizabeth Salzmann

Illustrated by C. A. Nobens

Consulting Editor, Diane Craig, M.A./Reading Specialist

ABDO
Publishing Company

Published by ABDO Publishing Company, 4940 Viking Drive, Edina, Minnesota 55435.

Printed in the United States.

Credits
Edited by: Pam Price
Curriculum Coordinator: Nancy Tuminelly
Cover and Interior Design and Production: Mighty Media
Photo Credits: AbleStock, Corbis Images, Corel, ShutterStock

Library of Congress Cataloging-in-Publication Data

Salzmann, Mary Elizabeth, 1968-
    Humming hummingbird / Mary Elizabeth Salzmann; illustrated by Cheryl Ann Nobens.
        p. cm. -- (Fact & fiction. Critter chronicles)
    Summary: Hugo and Holly, twin hummingbirds, work to save money for tickets to a concert featuring their favorite performer, Ruben Rubythroat. Alternating pages provide facts about hummingbirds.
    ISBN 10 1-59928-442-1 (hardcover)
    ISBN 10 1-59928-443-X (paperback)

    ISBN 13 978-1-59928-442-2 (hardcover)
    ISBN 13 978-1-59928-443-9 (paperback)
    [1. Saving and investment--Fiction. 2. Twins--Fiction. 3. Hummingbirds--Fiction.] I. Nobens, C. A., ill.
II. Title. III. Series.

    PZ7.S15565Hum 2006
    [E]--dc22

                                                                                        2006005540

SandCastle Level: Fluent

SandCastle™ books are created by a professional team of educators, reading specialists, and content developers around five essential components—phonemic awareness, phonics, vocabulary, text comprehension, and fluency—to assist young readers as they develop reading skills and strategies and increase their general knowledge. All books are written, reviewed, and leveled for guided reading, early reading intervention, and Accelerated Reader® programs for use in shared, guided, and independent reading and writing activities to support a balanced approach to literacy instruction. The SandCastle™ series has four levels that correspond to early literacy development. The levels help teachers and parents select appropriate books for young readers.

Emerging Readers
(no flags)

Beginning Readers
(1 flag)

Transitional Readers
(2 flags)

Fluent Readers
(3 flags)

These levels are meant only as a guide. All levels are subject to change.

FACT & FICTION

This series provides early fluent readers the opportunity to develop reading comprehension strategies and increase fluency. These books are appropriate for guided, shared, and independent reading.

FACT The left-hand pages incorporate realistic photographs to enhance readers' understanding of informational text.

FICTION The right-hand pages engage readers with an entertaining, narrative story that is supported by whimsical illustrations.

The Fact and Fiction pages can be read separately to improve comprehension through questioning, predicting, making inferences, and summarizing. They can also be read side-by-side, in spreads, which encourages students to explore and examine different writing styles.

FACT OR FICTION? This fun quiz helps reinforce students' understanding of what is real and not real.

SPEED READ The text-only version of each section includes word-count rulers for fluency practice and assessment.

GLOSSARY Higher-level vocabulary and concepts are defined in the glossary.

SandCastle™ would like to hear from you.

Tell us your stories about reading this book. What was your favorite page? Was there something hard that you needed help with? Share the ups and downs of learning to read. To get posted on the ABDO Publishing Company Web site, send us an e-mail at:

sandcastle@abdopublishing.com

Hummingbirds usually lay two eggs at a time. The eggs are the size of coffee beans and take about two weeks to hatch.

Hugo is doing his homework when his twin
sister, Holly, bursts into his room. "Hugo!" she
squeals. "Ruben Rubythroat is giving a concert
to benefit the nestless next month!"

"Cool!" Hugo exclaims. "His humming album
is number one! Let's ask if we can go."

Hummingbirds have weak legs and tiny
feet that they use only to groom
themselves and perch. They don't walk
or hop.

Holly and Hugo run to the living room. "Mom! Dad!" they shout. "May we go to the Ruben Rubythroat concert? Please?"

"All the money is going to help the nestless," says Hugo, "so it's for a good cause."

"Yes, you can go," says their mother. "But you have to earn the money for the tickets."

7

The female hummingbird has sole responsibility for building the nest and caring for the eggs and chicks.

Holly and Hugo get part-time jobs. Holly egg-sits in the afternoons so that mother hummingbirds can leave their nests to get dinner.

9

Hummingbirds eat constantly during the day. They eat insects and nectar from flowers.

Hugo works weekends at Flower Finders. He helps older hummingbirds who can't see well find flowers that have good nectar.

When flying, hummingbirds can make
popping, whistling, and humming sounds
with their wings and tails.

Hugo and Holly open a savings account at Bird Bank and deposit the money they make each week. "We'll have enough for the concert tickets in no time!" Hugo says, popping his tail happily.

BIRD BANK
FLY-THRU LANE

13

The hummingbird is the smallest bird and is the only bird that can hover in the air and fly backward.

In the evenings, Holly and Hugo do their homework quickly. Hugo says, "Mom said that since we're done with our homework, we can check out Ruben's Web site."

Holly hovers next to Hugo to look at the computer. "Oh!" she sighs. "Isn't he dreamy?"

FAN SITE

Ruben Rubythroat

Hummingbirds have long beaks with even longer tongues that they stick deep into flowers to drink nectar.

Finally it's the day of the concert. Holly and Hugo take the money from their savings account to pay for the tickets. They even have enough left over to share a delicious strawberry shake before the show.

Male hummingbirds attract mates by flying in spectacular acrobatic displays.

Hugo and Holly clap and cheer along with the
rest of the fans when Ruben comes on stage.
His backup birds dive and swoop all around him.
"Thank you all for coming tonight and helping
raise money for the nestless," he croons. "This
one's for you."

FACT OR FICTION?

Read each statement below. Then decide whether it's from the FACT section or the FICTION section!

1. Hummingbirds have weak legs.

2. Hummingbirds eat constantly.

3. Hummingbirds save money in banks.

4. Hummingbirds go to concerts.

ANSWERS
1. fact 2. fact 3. fiction 4. fiction

Hummingbirds usually lay two eggs at a time. The 9
eggs are the size of coffee beans and take about two 20
weeks to hatch. 23

Hummingbirds have weak legs and tiny feet that 31
they use only to groom themselves and perch. They 40
don't walk or hop. 44

The female hummingbird has sole responsibility for 51
building the nest and caring for the eggs and chicks. 61

Hummingbirds eat constantly during the day. They 68
eat insects and nectar from flowers. 74

When flying, hummingbirds can make popping, 80
whistling, and humming sounds with their wings and 88
tails. 89

The hummingbird is the smallest bird and is the 98
only bird that can hover in the air and fly backward. 109

Hummingbirds have long beaks with even longer 116
tongues that they stick deep into flowers to drink nectar. 126

Male hummingbirds attract mates by flying in 133
spectacular acrobatic displays. 136

Hugo is doing his homework when his twin | 8
sister, Holly, bursts into his room. "Hugo!" she | 16
squeals. "Ruben Rubythroat is giving a concert to | 24
benefit the nestless next month!" | 29

"Cool!" Hugo exclaims. "His humming album | 35
is number one! Let's ask if we can go." | 44

Holly and Hugo run to the living room. | 52
"Mom! Dad!" they shout. "May we go to the | 61
Ruben Rubythroat concert? Please?" | 65

"All the money is going to help the nestless," | 74
says Hugo, "so it's for a good cause." | 82

"Yes, you can go," says their mother. "But you | 91
have to earn the money for the tickets." | 99

Holly and Hugo get part-time jobs. Holly | 107
egg-sits in the afternoons so that mother | 115
hummingbirds can leave their nests to get dinner. | 123

Hugo works weekends at Flower Finders. He | 130
helps older hummingbirds who can't see well | 137
find flowers that have good nectar. | 143

Hugo and Holly open a savings account at Bird Bank and deposit the money they make each week. "We'll have enough for the concert tickets in no time!" Hugo says, popping his tail happily.

In the evenings, Holly and Hugo do their homework quickly. Hugo says, "Mom said that since we're done with our homework, we can check out Ruben's Web site."

Holly hovers next to Hugo to look at the computer. "Oh!" she sighs. "Isn't he dreamy?"

Finally it's the day of the concert. Holly and Hugo take the money from their savings account to pay for the tickets. They even have enough left over to share a delicious strawberry shake before the show.

Hugo and Holly clap and cheer along with the rest of the fans when Ruben comes on stage. His backup birds dive and swoop all around him. "Thank you all for coming tonight and helping raise money for the nestless," he croons. "This one's for you."

GLOSSARY

acrobatic. involving actions that require skill, energy, balance, and agility

benefit. to provide money or goods to help others

hover. to stay in one place in the air

nectar. a sweet liquid given off by plants

perch. to sit or stand on the edge of something

responsibility. a job or duty that must be done

shake. short for milk shake, a blended drink made of milk, flavoring, and, usually, ice cream

sole. being the only one

spectacular. very impressive or remarkable

To see a complete list of SandCastle™ books and other nonfiction titles from ABDO Publishing Company, visit **www.abdopublishing.com** or contact us at: 4940 Viking Drive, Edina, Minnesota 55435 • 1-800-800-1312 • fax: 1-952-831-1632